WOLF AND RAY

BARTŁOMIEJ GAJOWIEC

ILLUSTRATED BY LIUDMYLA BAGINSKA

Balboa Press books may be ordered through booksellers or by contacting:

Balboa Press
A Division of Hay House
1663 Liberty Drive
Bloomington, IN 47403
www.balboapress.com
844-682-1282

Because of the dynamic nature of the Internet, any web addresses or links contained in this book may have changed since publication and may no longer be valid. The views expressed in this work are solely those of the author and do not necessarily reflect the views of the publisher, and the publisher hereby disclaims any responsibility for them.

ISBN: 978-1-9822-6709-4 (sc)
ISBN: 978-1-9822-6708-7 (e)

Library of Congress Control Number: 2021907279

Print information available on the last page.

Balboa Press rev. date: 04/09/2021

BALBOA.PRESS
A DIVISION OF HAY HOUSE

WOLF AND RAY

It was Wednesday, or Saturday. No-one remembers it now, and anyway, why should we bother about details. They are not important. On that day, like every day at dawn, the Wolf was asleep in a small glade in the forest. Last evening, he made a lair for himself on the moss, right under a tall birch tree which was slowly beginning to shed small leaves. Autumn was on its way. Morning was slowly breaking over the forest, it was getting brighter and brighter. The early birds were singing and tidying up their nests after the night has come to an end. The woodpecker woke up and reckoned that it heard a worm in the bark, right under its nest hole. It took a lot of effort to excavate a hole in the tree big enough to shelter itself and the two little chicks. A beautiful grass snake also woke up. It slithered slowly from below a heap of leaves and looked around searching for light.

The Wolf opened his eyes but was not moving yet. He pricked up his ears, listening to the sounds of the morning forest. He recognized them perfectly well. He could tell what the animals were doing, what was going on in what part of the forest, who was awake and who was having a lie in. He has not yet sensed the almost inaudible flapping of the wings of his friend, the butterfly. Sometimes the butterfly came to meet the Wolf and used to sit on his nose while the Wolf patiently waited through its gentle tickling and looked at the patterns on the butterfly's wings. A little chamois who used to jump across the forest in the morning and who was always all over the place, was also asleep. It used to approach all animals and talk about everything. But, most importantly, the Wolf was looking for the Ray. He waited for it to appear on the glade, shining through a cloud, or tried to spot it from a distance when it was leaping from leaf to leaf.

Ray and the Wolf loved each other very much. They would do anything in the forest! They would run to the pond to look at their reflections in the calm water which was taking rest there.

They would jump across the stream which was gushing over the rocks sitting in its bed.

Sometimes Ray would hide from the Wolf who was then searching for his friend intensely, with focus typical of wolves

Sometimes some animal would try to hurt Ray. His light was so intense so it revealed a lot in the darkness of forest and for many it was far too much. So Wolf came usually with help showing his sharp teeth to keep the invader at bay. Sometimes he was forced to fight for his little Friend. So he did in total silence because that is how wolves fight to keep their thoughts in order. Afterwards Ray and Wolf would get back to their very places to rest a bit and warm the dark fur in sunlight.

"Something is wrong- the Wolf thought- Ray should already be here." He looked in the direction from which Ray used to come, but saw nothing but emptiness. A dark and cold emptiness which swallows everything that is good, and Ray IS good. The Wolf shook scraps of leaves off his fur and set off to find his friend. "If need be" – he thought - "I will fight for you again. If anyone has harmed you so you could not come here - I will stop him on his way." The animal set off towards the stream. He was all eyes and ears.

The stream was full of life-giving water which was never asleep. Even in the dark of the night. It kept thinking and chatting, even when the forest was asleep and no-one was listening.

The water saw so much and knew so much that the animals walked up every morning to look at its surface and learn the truth about things which made them curious or anxious. And the water would whisper to each and every animal about how things were. Looking at their reflections in the water, the animals were staring into their own yes and usually found their answers there. After all, the answers live at the bottom of the soul and you can look into the soul through the eyes. A few animals already gathered close to the stream. On seeing the Wolf the animals shifted restlessly, clearly worried. The Wolf had bad reputation in the forest. Some were afraid of him and some told strange and scary tales about him but nobody really knew him. And suddenly he was right there, as if out of nowhere, so full of life, so agile, with honey-colored eyes, alert to everything that was going on around him.

Before long, he sat on a big, moss-covered rock and howled - "Ray ! ! ! ! ! ! ! ! Where are you???" His voice could be heard throughout the forest. Animals stopped and looked in the direction from which the howling came. Some of them were scared and fled to their hiding places. Others, such as the big and strong bear, only nodded. "The Wolf is worried" - thought the bear - "He gives a howl like this when something hurts him." The bear knew the Wolf. They shared the forest between themselves. It was their home from time immemorial. The bear knew the strong legs and sharp teeth of the Wolf. It knew how much courage there was in the furry warrior. The Wolf watched the forest from the rock on which he was sitting, but Ray was nowhere to be found. He must have lost his way or fell into a trap - the Wolf thought. Ray is very young and does not know or understand many things. He is a tiny baby ray yet. I will find him even if I have to go to the end of the world" - he decided.

The wolf came up to the stream and put his mouth in the water. When he stopped drinking, he waited until the surface became flat and reflected his own face." Water, water, do you know what happened to my Ray?" asked the Wolf- "Have you seen him yet?" The water was murmuring but did not reflect any light. "No, I have not seen him" - the water said after a while. - "I am also worried about him. Go and find him, Wolf, and when you do - bring him here so I can enjoy his warmth. If I see him first, I will send birds to bring you the message or I will ask my softest dream to run to you and whisper the good news in your ear." The Wolf tucked his tail, as if resigned, and walked away towards the forest.

He jumped off the rock and ran to the east, where no forest animal has ever been. He ran and ran. He was brushing against shrubs which were trying to stop him. He jumped over ditches full of frogs croaking in small puddles. He ran across roads which were cut in the forest by people and was looking around carefully to avoid meeting any of them. People did not like wolves and he did not understand why. So he preferred to stay away from them. That was what his instinct told him, and what he heard from his ancestors. He passed round fallen trees and jumped over branches. From time to time he stopped and looked around carefully. He listened hoping to find even a tiniest trace of his beloved Ray. But Ray was not there. All of a sudden he caught a glimpse of the familiar light. "Here he is!" -he thought happily. -"I found him". But this was only a brief moment. The flash disappeared sooner than it appeared. Then again, something flashed and disappeared. "Ray was caught in a trap made by bad people" - the Wolf thought - "and cannot get away from it. He is not strong enough to cope by himself. But where is he???" The Wolf was running in the forest, howling, whining, sniffing trees, paths, tracks, looked for any sparkle. He was thrashing about and did not know which way to go. He was getting more and more tired. He has not eaten yet and his paws started to hurt. "I will do it" - he said to himself- "I will find him.". But he was getting more and more exhausted. "I need to drink some water now" - he thought and pricked his ears, to hear the sound of the stream. After a while he was dashing towards the familiar sound. By the water he was to find a surprise.

A beautiful, noble Crane was standing by the water. The long-legged bird in red head wear was the teacher and sage in the forest. If you were in trouble and had no clue what to do, you could always visit the Crane. It listened to you in stillness, looked deeply into your eyes and came up with the best solution. No animal could remember that the Crane was ever wrong. The Wolf ran up to the water and was drinking thirstily.

His fur was ruffled, with tiny beads of sweat, which, however, did not shine. It was Ray that used to play with them and shine its light on them. But Ray was not there. When the Wolf stopped drinking he looked at the Crane which was staring steadily into the water. "Can you see it?"- said the Crane unexpectedly. "What?"- the Wolf was surprised. "Everything that can be found there" - added the Crane in his mysterious way - "yourself, the world, the truth, lies, day and night, good and evil, everything is reflected in water. Water accepts all this, washes it, and returns it better and purer. Water is so soft yet, strangely, it can be as hard as a rock when it freezes. It is fragrant in spring, flowering in summer and in winter separates itself from the world with ice. See, it is so wise."

"I need your help, bird"- the Wolf broke in. "My dearest Ray got lost somewhere. He did not come to the forest today, did not shed any light over my glade and did not play hide and seek with me. He always comes, something must have happened to him. I am so upset". The Crane looked at the Wolf and it seemed to him that he saw tears in the Wolfs honey- coloured eyes. Or maybe it was an illusion? No-one can tell now. The Wolf, tired, lay down on the grass, put his head on his paws and looked at the bird which reached to one of its wings and produced a long, graphite black feather. The Crane held it in its beak, dipped it in the stream for a while and then gave it to the Wolf, saying: - "Take this feather and go and find Ray."

The Wolf was again running across hollows, jumping over rocks, steering clear of spiky branches to avoid sharp thorns. He rushed forward with all his might until he reached the edge of the forest. He had no clue what was ahead. He did not know any other world than the forest. But he was not afraid to face up to the unknown because he was going to find Ray. At some point he looked down a gorge which used to be a river bed but now was overgrown with thicket, unknown to the Wolf. He spotted light flashes, as if reflected in water. He ran to the bottom and between the thickets. They were stinging his nose and paws, others were scratching, but it was not important. The Wolf had a feeling that he would soon see the trap which might have kept his friend. He was right. In the middle of a dark meadow he saw an iron trap snapped shut. Inside he saw a tiny light. It was Ray, or rather his glowing heart. The Wolf stopped and gave such a mighty, loud howl that the whole forest shuddered. It cut the air as with a sharp sword, it could be heard everywhere. The Wolf looked up and saw the Crane soaring in the sky. The bird was circling above his head. The Crane was watching. The Wolf bent down and scrutinized the trap. Ray was looking at his friend in pain, but trustfully. He knew that he would be safe now and would suffer no harm.

The Wolf took the jaws of the trap in his teeth, braced his feet against the ground and turned his head with all the strength he could gather to tug the iron jaws apart and let Ray go. "Get out"- he growled through his teeth closed on the trap. Ray slowly but obediently crawled away from the cold iron. The Wolf opened his jaws and the trap loudly snapped shut again. He bent with tender care over Ray and asked, breathing heavily" What happened to you? Why are you here? I was worried about you. My glade is dark without you ... " Ray looked in the Wolfs eyes and told him his story. In a meantime the Wolf was licking turf and dirt off Ray's body and the little drop, which he thought to be blood, but was not sure if rays have blood.

No one heard the story. We do not know when and why Ray was caught in the trap. We may only guess that something bad happened to him. That someone whose heart is eaten away by his light decided to take this light away from him and led him along a path which the little Ray could not recognize and see it was dangerous. The Crane was still circling above when it saw the Wolf and Ray coming out of the thickets. Ray, shining with its full light, suddenly shot high up in the sky. It ran close to the Crane giving it a soft and grateful kiss, because he knew the Crane helped him so much. Then it dropped again next to the Wolf, snuggled itself in its fur and they both went slowly towards their forest, towards their glade. The Wolf said - "We will visit the Water, to share our good news." But the Water already knew everything. It saw everything from the clouds because it was drops of rain. It saw everything from the Wolfs eyes because it was his tears. It saw everything from the darkness because it was mist. It saw and knew that the Wolf found Ray and Ray found the Wolf.

On the way to the glade they met the little Chamois who had always something to say and was always all over the place. Ray fiddled with its hooves, twinkled in its eyes and played on its back for a while. The Bear passed them by, giving friendly growls, he had already heard the good news from the Water. The Butterfly flew above their heads and the Wolf smiled happily. They were returning to the glade and Ray knew he would be safe now. As they were walking the Wolf was telling Ray what he saw on his way and how important it was now for Ray to know how to tell right from wrong. "You are the Light of my Glade" said the Wolf. Ray cuddled into the warm fur of the animal and they walked on together. Inseparably inseparable.

And this surely is no fairy tale any more.

Printed in the United States
by Baker & Taylor Publisher Services